W9-AOC-887

Tsunamis

Ted O'Hare

Bethany, Missouri

Photo Credits:
Cover © Courtesy U.S. Army/ Aaron Allmon II; Title Page © Christopher Waters; Pages 4-5 © Bridget Zawitoski; Page 6 © Libi Ostrovsky; Page 7 © Gregson Edwards, Andriy Rovenko; Page 9 © Jarvis Gray, Steven Collins; Page 10 © Micha Fleuren; Page 11 © James Hearn, A. S. Zain; Page 12 © Jarvis Gray; Page 15 © Paul Prescott, Norlisza Binti Azman; Page 17 © USGS; Page 19 © Mosista Pambundi; Pages 21, 22 © NOAA

Cataloging-in-Publication Data

O'Hare, Ted, 1961-
Tsunamis / Ted O'Hare. — 1st ed.
p. cm. — (Natural disasters)

Includes bibliographical references and index.
Summary: Illustrations and text introduce tsunamis,
from what they are, to their history, causes, and prediction.
ISBN-13: 978-1-4242-1403-7 (lib. bdg. : alk. paper)
ISBN-10: 1-4242-1403-3 (lib. bdg. : alk. paper)
ISBN-13: 978-1-4242-1493-8 (pbk. : alk. paper)
ISBN-10: 1-4242-1493-9 (pbk. : alk. paper)

1. Tsunamis—Juvenile literature. [1. Tsunamis.
2. Natural disasters.] I. O'Hare, Ted, 1961- II. Title.
III. Series.
GC221.5.O43 2007
551.46'37—dc22

First edition

802 N. 41st Street, P.O. Box 505
Bethany, MO 64424, U.S.A.
Printed in China
Library of Congress Control Number: 2006911283

Table of Contents

What Makes a Tsunami?

A **tsunami** is a wave, or series of waves, caused by the movement of water in the sea. Tsunami is a Japanese word that means "harbor wave."

Earthquakes, volcanic **eruptions**, **landslides**, and even meteorite impacts can cause tsunamis.

When a tsunami begins, the waves move away from the source. Some tsunamis can travel long distances. They may strike land thousands of miles from where they begin.

Tsunamis move with great speed, sometimes as much as 500 miles (800 kilometers) an hour.

Not all tsunamis are “towers” of water hitting the coastline. Many look like rising tides.

At sea, tsunamis are hard to detect because they seem flat. Only when tsunamis approach land do they begin to grow in height.

Before a tsunami hits land the water **recedes**. This exposes land that is normally under water. It is one of the few warning signs that a tsunami may be approaching.

Although tsunamis can strike anywhere, they are most common in the Pacific Ocean.

Earthquakes Under the Sea

Earthquakes under the sea are most often the cause of tsunamis. Sometimes the quake occurs 13,000 feet (4,000 meters) below sea level.

Undersea earthquakes move big rocks at the bottom of the ocean. This also means that a lot of water is **displaced**.

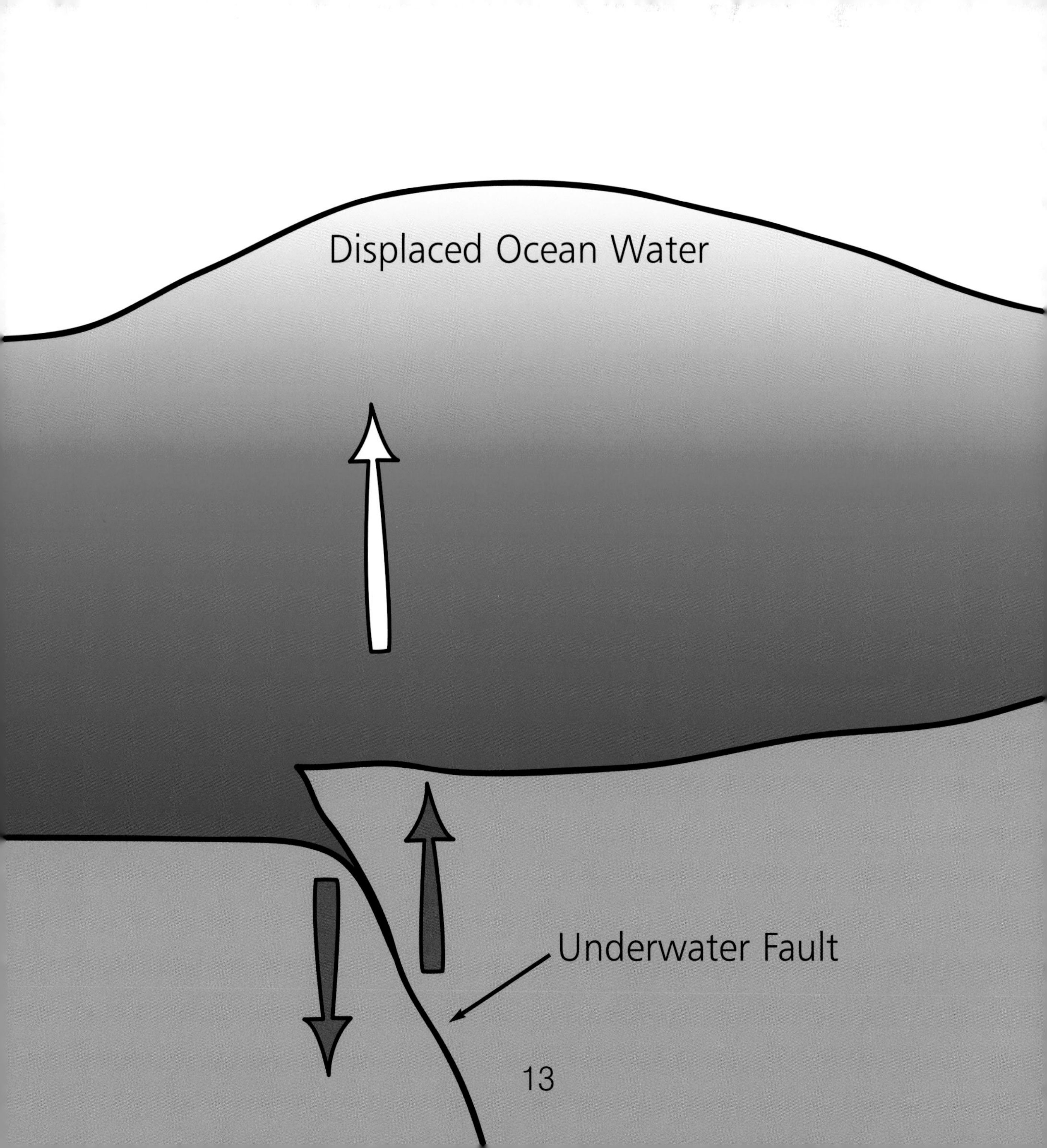
Displaced Ocean Water
Underwater Fault

On December 26, 2004, a huge tsunami struck many areas on the edge of the Indian Ocean. This tsunami was caused by a large undersea earthquake.

No one knows for sure, but it is believed that around 230,000 people died. The tsunami caused major damage to Indonesia, Sri Lanka, India, and Thailand, among other places. It is the most deadly tsunami ever known.

VEGA

Volcanic Tsunamis

Volcano eruptions also create tsunamis. Many of these eruptions also occur under the sea. Tsunamis can also be created by landslides caused by volcanic eruptions.

Famous Tsunamis

A famous tsunami took place in 1883 in Indonesia. It began with a volcanic eruption on the island of Krakatoa. It was so large that it could be heard more than 2,000 miles (3,219 kilometers) away.

A huge tsunami was the result. It caused more than 36,000 people to die.

Another famous, but less dangerous, tsunami struck Alaska in 1958. More than 90 million tons of rock slid into Lituya Bay. The tsunami it caused is the tallest recorded to date.

Not long after, in 1960, a terrible tsunami struck the coast of Chile. Thousands were swept out to sea and were killed.

NOAA
R 552

Predicting Tsunamis

With today's technology, tsunamis can sometimes be predicted. Scientists study and monitor the paths of undersea earthquakes. Early warning and evacuation can sometimes help to save lives.

Glossary

displaced (diss PLAYCD) — replaced or moved

earthquake (URTH qwayk) — a jolting of the Earth's surface

eruptions (ee RUP shunz) — explosions, often caused by volcanoes

landslides (LAND sliydz) — movements of earth and rock down a hillside

recedes (re SEEDZ) — to pull back

tsunami (soo NAHM ee) — a wave caused by movement of water in the sea

Index

FURTHER READING

Morris, Ann, and Heidi Larson. *Tsunami: Helping Each Other*. Lerner, 2005.
Orme, David and Helen. *Tsunamis.* Children's Press, 2005.
Walker, Niki. *Tsunami Alert*. Crabtree Publishing, 2006.

WEBSITES TO VISIT

Because Internet links change so often, Fitzgerald Books has developed an online list of websites related to the subject of this book. This site is updated regularly. Please use this link to access the list: www.fitzgeraldbookslinks.com/nd/tsu

ABOUT THE AUTHOR

Ted O'Hare is an author and editor of children's nonfiction books. Ted has written over fifty children's books over the past decade. Ted has worked for many publishing houses including the Macmillan Children's Book Group.